LOVE DIFFERENTLY

SNEHAL ARORA

Made with ❤ on the Notion Press Platform
www.notionpress.com

Contents

Preface

Snehal Arora

As a first time writer this book was once only a small idea that over the span of a few month became one of my most proud achievements. I wrote this book to help spread awareness about the LGBTQ Community and to bring forth their struggles. The book also helped me in learning more about the lives of the people who are a part of this community and their stories. This book helps me in not only writing about a topic that is close to my heart, but also give back to the community and fight for a cause.

Prologue

"Do you have any idea of what you have done?" Anger all over his face as walks closer to me. He shreds the letter I wrote to him, treating it as though it was nothing.

I wanted to run away, fight back, do anything to stop this. My vision was blurry and my limbs aching with bruises. I couldn't move and every part of me was hurting. His friends tower over me as I lay on the cold asphalt. I felt helpless as there was no escape. He gets closer sitting down to face me. One of his hands gripping my collar and the other one holding my face. His hands were cold and his grip too tight. He withdraws him hand from my face and pulls it back before his fist comes in contact with the side of my face. I wince in the pain, hoping it would come to an end.

"You're a pervert!" says one of his friends before kicking me in the stomach. "Stay away for us!"

The smell of blood and cement overpowers my senses. Each breath takes more energy than I have. I try to keep my eyes open, staying in control of my body. Soon I give in. I become numb to the kicks and punches, my eyelids slowly closing. I feel lifeless before I finally drift off.

♡♡♡

A bright light shines into my eyes almost blinding me. I blink a few times before realizing that I was in the hospital. My sister holding my hand in hers.

"Do Mom and Dad know?" I ask her, my voice cracking.

"They found out." She said softly, "They're outside right now, give them a little time to cool down."

"Do you think they'll accept me?" Even though I knew the answer I was hoping my sister would lie to me.

“Of course,” she says a small tear rolling down her eye.

From that day onwards, I had always kept my sexuality a secret, I couldn’t afford to tell someone else.

Love is Love.

It doesn't matter how...
It doesn't matter why...
It doesn't matter who...

1

A New Start

The room is pitch black. I keep walking forward trying to find an escape, but it's like I'm stuck in an endless corridor. I hear soft footsteps behind me, barely audible, as though someone was tiptoeing. I turn around slowly, my heart racing and my hand shaking. The corridor was still dark, but I could somehow make out a silhouette running away from me. I walked towards it, each step as careful and as quiet as can be. As I continue forward, I see a dim light shining through a small window, like a small glimmer of hope. I run towards it, pushing my fears aside. I can still feel the silhouette around me, like a spirit that is hovering. My breath gets more erratic and my feet more desperate to reach the escape. Until I can't stop, I'm running in the direction of the window, but I can't control my feet. I have to stop. As I get closer my feet start running faster, and I lose more and more control of my body. I step on the ledge of the window and jump down to the darkness beneath. This feels like the end, my last breath. As I continue falling, I look back at the window, only to be stared back at by the stone-cold faces of my parents. They don't move a muscle. I reach out my hand asking for help, but there wasn't even the slightest change in their expression.

I finally open my eyes. The bright light from the sun almost blinds me before I can take in my surroundings. I don't know whether it was the nightmare or the heat that caused beads of sweat to form. I bury my head in my hands trying not to replay the dream in my mind.

"Are you okay?" asks my sister, a worried expression painted across her face.

"Yeah" I reply trying to calm myself, "just a bad dream."

My parents sit in the front of the small 4-seater car. They look back to see what happened but couldn't care less about my troubles. To them I had always been invisible, the child they didn't want. We were currently moving to a new city, to get a fresh start, but it felt like I was running away from the past. The journey so far had been highways and grey buildings, the only source of entertainment in the car was the static radio. We had never been a family that would play games together or talk about our lives, but rather only conversing when it was required.

Soon we entered a lively neighbourhood, one where the houses were bright, and the sidewalks filled with people. It was much different from where I had grown up, but looking at how happy the people there were, I felt like this might actually be a good change.

♡♡♡

Home. It's the one place we all feel like we belong, it's that feeling of comfort and ease. But here I was thousands of miles away from the place I called home. I stared out of the window in my room, looking at the unfamiliar environment surrounding me.

"Noah!" called out Nia, "These boxes aren't going to unpack themselves."

Like any other older sibling, Nia was always telling me what to do, she was like a third parent to me. The only difference was I loved her more than I could ever love them. She was the one that raised me, my parents were only there to point out all my mistakes. We shared the same brown eyes and tanned skin, but other than that we were worlds apart. She was always the perfect child, the one responsible one who never did anything wrong. I always wanted to be like her, to be normal.

"Why don't you take this box to the kitchen and start unpacking." She says motioning towards a box labelled 'Kitchen.'

I set the box on top of the counter and start sorting through the contents. My mother enters the kitchen, walking past me. As though by instinct, I my entire body freezes. I stare at the ground, looking at the white marble tiles hoping they would somehow absorb me. I always envied people who were close to their parents, mine never liked me. The worst part was they didn't even try to hide it.

I can feel my mother's eye on me, analysing and criticizing me. "Nia, you're responsible for taking Noah to school tomorrow."

That's all she says before leaving. I take a deep breath in, and my entire body relaxes. I always hated that I was a burden on my sister, I would always blame myself for her having to look after me. But a small part of myself blamed it on them, she only had to be there because they couldn't be.

Nia walks into the kitchen carrying another box. "Why don't you leave this, I'll do it."

"It's okay, I'm happy to help-"

"You need to get some rest before tomorrow."

2 Him

As I walk into school, I have my eye fixated on the brick floor. This day has barely started, and I am already wishing that it would end. As I head over to my first class I try and avoid everybody, hoping that I would somehow disappear. I walk into class and look around to find the most secluded seat. My laptop is opened in front of me, as I start scrolling through the timetable for today, trying to memorize the rooms that I have to go to. I was hoping to be able to get through today without any human interactions, but I couldn't even get through the first class.

"Hey!" I look up at the source of the voice, staring straight into his brown eyes. They weren't the usual brown colour; his eyes were lighter, almost a shade of hazel. I stare at them for longer than I should have but I can't stop looking. "Do you mind if I sit here?"

"No, of course not." I forced my eyes to look straight at the computer screen in front of me, while he made himself comfortable in the chair next to mine. I wanted to look at him. I wanted to stare at him for hours. I wanted to hear his voice again. But most of all I wanted to forget he existed. I was doing it again, having feelings I wasn't allowed to.

My parents would have killed me if they could hear my thoughts right now.

"Are you new here?" He looks directly at me, and I suddenly feel uncomfortable. "Haven't seen you around before."

"Yeah, it's my first day."

"I'm Mark," he says reaching out a hand towards me.

"My name is Noah." I shake his hand, hating how nervous I was around him. My parents voice echoed in my brain, 'You have to get over this phase. It's not normal to be feeling this way.' They always told me bury my feelings and never look back, to become someone who was accepted by society and was considered to be a part of it. They always told me to be someone else, and here I was failing to meet their expectations.

Just then the first bell rang. I start packing up my thing to leave, trying my best to ignore him. "I'll see you around." He said with a small smile on his face before walking out.

Sexuality has always been a clear-cut conversation in India, girls for boys and boys for girls. That is also what I knew growing up. The first time I saw a same gender relationship, I was like, oh cool, that can happen too, I guess. I didn't think much of it as a 9–10-year-old, it just didn't seem like a big deal to me. Over time I realised that I also maybe liked girls. Again, I didn't think much of it, you don't think much about these things at a young age, they seem insignificant. But recently, I do find myself wondering how I would define myself; I like girls so I'm not, 'straight' but I also still like boys so I'm also not 'gay'. I like both genders but not regardless of what they are so I'm not 'pansexual', and I don't feel equally towards both so I'm not 'bisexual'. I felt so caught up between the labels that have been established by our society that I forget, first and foremost come our own

feelings and emotions. I have discovered recently that sexuality does not have to know the confines of labels. Everyone feels differently and this should not be restricted by labels.

The rest of the day flew by. Nobody else came up to me or tried talking to me, and I can't say that I wasn't glad. But the lesson that I feared the most was here. Lunch. I was worried about having to talk to people, but it seemed like everyone was in their own world. I took a small portion of food and sat down in a lonely corner table.

"Looks like you've made a lot of friends on your first day."

A small smile creeps up on my face as I see him stand there. His dirty blonde hair looks dishevelled, and yet seems to be perfect. I wish I wasn't happy to see him, but deep down I know that no matter how hard I try I won't be able to get rid of these feelings. I just wish others would understand that too.

"Quite judgemental from someone who's always alone," I reply.

"Ouch," he says before setting his plate down next to me. I already knew that things would go wrong between us. But I wanted to enjoy the journey before I have to reach the destination.

Before I can start eating a few kids in our grade start laughing as they walk past us. "Looks like the gay kid found a friend!" I hear one of them say. Fear started to grow inside me. How would they know? Who told them? What were they going to do to me? My grip around my spoon tightens, my knuckles turning white. Suddenly one of them spills their glass of water on Mark. That's when I realized they weren't talking about me, they were teasing Mark. My hand curled into tight fists and my jaw clenched, I wanted to kill every last one of them. I knew what it felt like to be in his place. To have people treat you differently, to not be able to fit in no matter how hard you try. I didn't know it would hurt more seeing him go through this.

3

Our Spot

There are flashing lights everywhere, and the entire world seems to be a blur. I realize that I'm trapped in a car. The seat belt around my chest gets tighter every moment. I try opening the door, but it seems to be jammed. I look around the car, there's nobody there. I sit in the passenger seat, while the car speeds forward on a deserted road. I try to find an escape, but the car continues to speed up. My hands tremble as the vehicle starts moving at 100 miles per hour. My body starts to freeze in fear, and I lose control of my limbs. I am powerless, like a bird trapped in a cage. I curl my hands into fists and shut my eyes close as I try to escape this nightmare. When I open my eyes, all I could see was the barren land that we were passing and the cold empty car. The temperature starts to drop, and I have nothing to keep me warm. The air gets thicker with fog, and dew starts settling on the windows making it harder to see the path ahead. But that seems like the least of my problems when I realize that the road is ending. It was now that I could see that the empty road was leading straight into a cliff. I wanted to scream for help, to break through this car, but I was still unable to move. I brace myself for the fall as the car leaves the road. Everything turns black. Every inch of my body hurts. Every second feels like a year as I wait for the end. But I survive. I look towards the driver's seat, the once empty seat that was occupied by a ghost driver, is now where my sister lays. Her hands are on the steering wheel, blood dripping down her face, and her entire body seems to be broken. I did this. I hurt her.

I wake up from yet other nightmare, hair soaking from sweat and my throat dry. They started a few years back, and usually most of them aren't that bad, but I still wish I would be able to get a few hours of sleep before I have to deal with everything going on. I never told anyone about them, even if I wanted to I couldn't. Nia was the only one who would actually listen to me, but telling her about having nightmares would only make her worry. I get up from my bed and walk towards my window. Even though I'm still getting used to the new room, my window is something that helps calming me. It allows me to look into the world, see the quiet streets and the moonlit houses, to imagine what life would be like if I was different. If I was normal.

"Can't sleep?" I almost jump when I hear the familiar voice.

"Mark?" There he was standing in my backyard. I didn't know if I was more mad or surprised.

I rushed downstairs. All I could think about was how much trouble I would be in if my parents saw him. A small part of me was glad he came, but I tried to bury that feeling as deep as I could. It's what I was always told to do. Hide the parts of me they didn't like. Pretend to be someone I wasn't.

"I was in the neighbourhood." He said when I finally reached him. "Thought I would drop in."

"You live in the neighbourhood." I replied, trying to get rid of him before he woke someone up. "You need to go, now."

"Come on." He looks at me with an innocent expression on his face. "Just this once, trust me."

A part of me knew this was wrong, that I was making the wrong decision. But just this one time, doing the wrong thing felt right. All I knew was that right now I could use a distraction, something that takes me away from everything going on at home. I nod my head slowly, still unsure of what I'm saying yes to.

"So, what is this place?" I look around, we stand in the middle of a jungle. The trees above us allows small streams of light onto the forest floor. The wind softly rustles the leaves, and the aroma of wet soil surrounds us.

"It's just a small place where I can escape." He looks around, taking in his surroundings. Looking at him like this makes me feel at ease, for a moment, I believe that nothing could go wrong. "You know how people have that one thing they are extremely attached to, something that they could never let go of. This place is that for me."

"So why did you bring me here?" I sit down on a small rock, looking up at the stars.

"I don't know." He sits down beside me, following my gaze. "This placed often calmed me, and you seemed to be extremely uptight."

"Also, I wanted to apologise for what happened at school." He says finally breaking the silence. "I would understand if you wanted me out of your life."

"What?" I was shocked. I knew that being treated like an outcast in school wasn't easy, but I wanted to help him, be there for him. Not run away, leaving him stranded. "I'm not leaving you just because of something that a couple of jerks said to you."

"You don't understand. It not just something they call me; it is who I am."

"I know what you're going through. My previous school, something similar happened to me." He looks at me with confusion. I shouldn't be telling him this. I wanted to keep my past a secret, I had to. But sitting here with him, I felt like I could trust him.

"A few years back I realised that I was gay. At first, I thought it was a phase, or just a small obsession with a guy. But I never really got rid of the way I feel. Back then my parents had been extremely supportive of what I do, so thought they would understand this as well."

"Did you come out to them?" He asks.

"Not directly. I liked this boy, his name was Austin. We were quite close, and one day I decided to take a chance. I wrote him a small letter, telling him about the way I felt. I still regret doing that. Turns out not only did he not like me back, but he was also extremely homophobic. Soon the entire school knew my sexuality and they were less than welcoming about it. And when I thought things couldn't get any worse, the news somehow reached my parents. They were furious when they found out. I was grounded for almost a month and told that I had to stop being gay. From that day onwards they've never talked to me."

He shifts a little closer to me. His head resting on my shoulder. I feel much better knowing that even though I told him everything he won't go anywhere. We sat there in the silence, but it wasn't uncomfortable, in fact it was the most relaxed I had been in a long time. I felt like a weight had been lifted off my chest, like there was one person that I didn't have to pretend for.

4

Pride Club

"Where are we going?" I look around as he led me down a narrow path through the trees. It was a Saturday night and somehow Mark had gotten me to leave my house again. I had to lie to my parents and Nia, even though I wanted nothing more than to be able to tell them the truth. In more ways than one, moving here had turned out to be better than I expected.

"I want you to meet a few people," he says, "Come on!"

We walk on the path for a few more minutes before I finally see a dim light coming from a building. As we get closer, I realize we are on our way to school. Except it wasn't filled with noisy strangers or dumb teenagers, it looked calm under the moonlight.

"Hate to break it to you, but school doesn't start for another 10 hours."

"Better early than late." He says with a smirk on his face.

He carries on walking, the path getting clearer as we get closer. We head straight inside school, and after a few turns around hallways, we reach the only classroom that has the light on. I could hear people inside, talking and discussing something.

"Listen, here you don't have to be someone else." He looked at me, "they're going to accept you just the way you are."

Usually meeting new people was something I avoided, but knowing that he trusted them, somehow made it easier. I didn't know what to expect when he opened the door, but seeing rainbow decorations and people having a small party, was definitely not it. It seemed to be like a small pride celebration, people escaping the world to embrace who they really were.

"Is this like a pride club?" I look around to see people wearing colourful clothing, and the seven colours of the rainbow in every corner.

"More like a gay bar minus the alcohol," he says leading me inside.

For me being queer now doesn't make too much for a difference in my life because now everyone's really understanding about it. Even though I haven't come out to my family yet I'm pretty sure my mom has a clue and she's okay with it and my father even though he's a bit homophobic I know that when I do come out, he wouldn't be angry or anything. Though I did feel weird about myself before I knew I might be queer because like everyone in 7th grade was having crushes on the opposite gender and since I have never had one, I felt a bit odd. And I guess sometimes I feel like I'm faking being queer because I still haven't had a crush and something like that but then I do feel like I'd rather be with a girl than a boy.

As I head back home, I feel much better. Moving to this new town was only me running away from past memories, instead of moving forward. Today, I was actually able to put my past aside and just be who I wanted to be. I was able to talk about who I liked without someone thinking I was abnormal. It felt good not to have to hide a part of yourself one because others didn't want to see it. I open the back door as quietly as I could, tiptoeing inside.

"Where have you been?" Hearing my sisters voice almost gives me a heart attack. She stands in front of me, with her arms crossed. She looks at me with stone cold eyes, and guilt immediately starts to fill up inside me.

"I was just out with a couple of friends." I say defensively.

"You can't just sneak out like that." She finally relaxes. "At least tell me when you plan on leaving the house." It felt nice to have someone who still cared about me, even if it meant getting scolded.

"I went to a pride meeting." I blurt out. I wasn't going to hide it from her, I just didn't know the right time to tell her. She had always supported me, but I was afraid that she wouldn't want me to be telling everyone about my sexuality again.

"How was it?" Her expression changed completely; she was now grinning a little.

"It was actually pretty good, I got to meet a lot of new people. It felt nice to just be who I was." I say, remembering how the people I met and the stories I heard. "I was finally able to talk to others who knew what I was going through."

"Look, I don't want to crush your spirits but be careful. I'm happy that you've finally found a safe space. I just don't want you to go through what happened last time, and I don't even want to think about what mom and dad will do if the find out." She places her hand on my shoulder. I know that she was looking out for me but hearing everything that could go wrong makes me doubt my decisions.

5

Confessions and Threats

I didn't know how I got to this point. I never put too much thought in who I actually liked, was it a girl, was it a boy. At first, I just went along with the societal norms. I still can't define my sexuality, but I feel deep inside I know what it is. There was something. A feeling. An attraction. I just didn't have the time to think about what it could be or think things through, and figuring out that part of me was just too much. So, I just went along with a flow. It definitely brought me closer to my friends and meet new people, and accepting myself helped me in finding a part of myself. After just labelling it as 'I don't know', I was just relieved of stress and just had fun. I was able to try from both worlds and just admitted at the fact that something was there for sure, I didn't know what it was yet.

It had been a few weeks since I first met Mark, and now we spent most of our time together. He was the first person I would meet in the morning and the last person I would talk to when we snuck out for the pride club meetings, plus any free time I had I would run off to our spot in the woods. It seemed as though I would spend every day with him, and they were some of the most enjoyable times. Things at home were pretty much the same, and it was nice to have an escape from all of that.

"Aren't you here a little too soon?" I ask walking out to the yard where he was waiting for me.

"Something happened at home, and I just wanted to get away from it. So, I came here. If you want, I come again a little later."

"No, it's okay." We start walking towards school as usual, but today something was different. Mark wasn't himself, he looked as though someone had sucked the life out of him. "Better early than late, right?" I said trying to cheer him up. All I got in return was a solemn nod.

"Can I ask what happened?" I didn't want to pry but seeing how blue he looked I wanted to do anything that I could to help him.

"It's my father. He doesn't know I'm gay. I was helping him out with some work at home, when news started showing some clips of a pride parade." He looks down at his feet as we walk. I could tell that this made him uncomfortable, but I was glad he was opening up to me. "He started with his homophobic behaviour again. I know he wasn't talking about me but the way he hates the gay community makes it difficult to be around him. It's like I'm walking on eggshells when I'm with him, trying to act as straight as possible because he would probably kill me if he found out. Every time I leave the house to meet you it's like I can finally take a breath. I guess that why I came to your house without thinking."

"You can come to my place whenever you want. Having to spend time with you isn't all that bad." We look at each other and share a soft smile. His hand reaches for mine, and subconsciously I hold it. The warmth of his hand and the cold breeze in the forest, this was all I ever wanted. In this moment, I knew that no matter what happened I would always have him by my side. He had helped me when I was ready to give up, knowing that I was of some support to him was reassuring. I was always afraid of being a burden on the people who were there for me, but he never once made me feel like I wasn't needed or wanted.

We were in close proximity of the school when we started hearing crashes and the braking of glass. As if on instinct both of us started running towards the noise. There was chaos everywhere, people I knew from the pride club were standing outside the school, some injured and others panicking. I could see people frantically calling 911 and trying to get help. The window of the room where we held the meetings was broken, and shattered glass lay everywhere.

"What happened here?" Mark asks someone who had a glass shard in his arm.

"Some of the seniors threw a brick through the window. They found out about the meetings and decided to take matters into their hands." Anger grew inside me. Society always thought of us as criminals or the villains. Like they would be better off if they got rid of all the gays or need to take action against us. I hated that loving the type of person that I wanted to love was something that they should be able to decide.

Me and Mark rush in to help anyone who was injured. The room was a mess, once filled with fun discussions and happiness now had blood and pain. I started hearing the police and ambulance sirens, it was a relief knowing help was here. This wasn't the first time I had been a witness to hate crime, but every time it happened it would give me another reason to hide my sexuality. Thankfully no one was seriously injured and by the time everyone was given medical attention the situation was under control. Although nobody knew exactly who did this the detectives were trying to find answers.

“Noah! What are you doing here?!” I froze, it was my parents. Just when I thought things couldn’t get worse. I keep my head down as I walk towards them, preparing for the punishment they had in mind. “I can’t believe you would lie to us and join some disgraceful club!” my mother said, the least bit concerned about if something had happened to me. My father grabs my arm and drags me towards the car. His grip piercing my skin, but I keep quiet. Even Nia wasn’t here to help me.

“The next time I see you in some gay club or even talking to one of these children will be the last day you sleep under my roof.” My father’s threat rings in my ears, and fear taking control of my body.

6

Bittersweet Goodbyes

Ever since that day things just got worse. I avoided everyone from the pride club as much as I could, but the hardest part was not talking to him. I would reach school late everyday to avoid seeing him in the first lesson and never entering the cafeteria during lunch. When I saw him in the corridors or outside school, a part of me wanted to forget everything and just go to him. To freeze the world around us so that I could be with him, even if it wasn't possible. I missed our spot in the forest, the moonlight, the earthy smell, and the feeling of escaping the hectic life for peace in nature. Without him life was monotonous, the same grey walls of school, but he somehow added colour to them. Opening the door to my first lesson I had expected the class to be empty. But instead, I walk in and stare into his eyes, I should run away, hide, anything but stand as still as a statue, in front of him.

"Have you been ignoring me?" He asks me. Hurt visible on his face, and I knew I was the one that caused it. Seeing him look so vulnerable and real caught me off guard, it was all my fault, I shouldn't have gotten close to him. I shouldn't have loved him because it only ruins both of us.

"I've been busy," I say looking anywhere but toward him.

I want to comfort him, to tell him that I'm always going to be there for him. Right now, I just don't know how to. I'm afraid telling him the truth would pull us apart and lying would only make everything worse. I know running away from my problems isn't the best way to solve them but right now I needed to be as far away from him as I could be.

"I thought we were going to be honest with each other." He moves closer to me. I don't know whether I want to push him away and never look back again or close the gap and tell him that I won't be able to live without him.

"It's my parents. They have always hated me for not being attracted to the opposite gender. Right now, I'm in a mess, and I don't know what to do. They might even disown me if the see us together, that doesn't mean I'm trying to avoid you it just means that it's probably for the best if there's a little distance between us." I try explaining my situation to him, but he only seems to be more confused.

"Distance? Noah, you're the only one who doesn't run away, attack or tease me every time I see you, and you want distance between us. You're the only one I talk to about every aspect of my life and now you just walk away like it was nothing. This might sound selfish, but I really needed you, as a friend if nothing else." He walks away, irritated by what I had just told him. It was my fault. I decided that this was enough, I didn't want to live by my parents' rules anymore.

7

Gone

The dark forest surrounds me, intimidating trees, harsh winds, and an unsettling ground. I walk where the narrow trail leads me, each step almost being my last one. As I continue, I see a silhouette, a guy sitting on a small rock, his curly hair dancing in the wind. I realize that its him. He looks peaceful sitting there, like a calm soul resting. I shouldn't go near him, I shouldn't disturb his perfect state, but I continue to walk forward. That when something stops me. A vine wrapping around my left leg pulling me back. The vine grows stronger and thicker as I try to pull away, almost digging through my flesh. Soon another vine reaches for my other leg, almost wrapping my lower half. I am trapped, with no way out. I want to call out to him, ask him for help, but the words don't leave my mouth. Instead, they are pushed further down my throat, suffocating me. By some miracle he looks back, his brown eyes staring into mine. My body relaxes a little knowing that he was here for me, but something feels off. His eyes don't look at me with the sparkle they had, instead they are now clouded with hatred. He runs off further into the darkness, leaving me alone. Although my limbs are currently being crushed by vines, the stinging in my heart hurt more that the physical pain.

I wake up the next morning, remembering the dream I had. It made me realize what I had to do. I had had enough of their conditions, their expectations, their opinions. I always felt like a disappointment because to them I wasn't anything but that. I couldn't believe that I left the few people who saw me as I was, for the people to whom I wasn't invisible. I even left him, the one I didn't want to imagine my life without, the one I was ready to give everything up for.

I'm Bisexual. I have always been confused about personality and finding who I am attracted to. Although my parents were supportive of any decisions I made about my identity, I could never understand what my limits were for my gender identity. I am glad that my parents are supportive, despite my sexuality. I have seen friends of mine not being able to tell their parents about their sexuality, because they aren't as understanding or considerate as mine. I guess it was always conflicting that I would be attracted to both guys and girls, and for a long time I struggled figuring it out. I finally realized that it wasn't always one gender or the other, and that I could be attracted to both.

"I need to talk to you," I say looking at my parents, "both of you."

"We're busy, Noah. Whatever it is Nia can help you," answers my mother walking out on me once again.

"Just this once can you look at me like I'm not a complete disappointment. I know I'm not the child you wanted, or the normal son you expected, but it really isn't my fault." My mother stops in her tracks. She looks at me as though she saw a ghost. I don't blame her, I myself would not have thought that someday I would have the courage to talk back or take a stand for myself. I take a breath as I choose my next words carefully.

"I have never been attracted to a girl in my entire life. I know you're confused as to why, but the truth is I don't know. All I know it's not something I could change, or something I would even want to change. And before you say anything, no this is not a temporary feeling, and I am not trying to be someone else. When we left our old home, I thought I could forget about the past, try to be someone who you guys would be more accepting of. I can't do it anymore. I can't hide the fact that I'm gay because I'm done hiding a part of myself. I don't expect you do be comfortable with all this cause even after 2 years you still treat me the same way. All I am asking is for you to allow me to go back to the pride club. I promise I will be careful; I'll make sure that history doesn't repeat itself."

"Noah, last time you decided to be bold and 'embrace yourself,' you ended up in the hospital," my mother said using air quotes. I hated that they blamed me for getting bullied, according to them I chose to be different even though I knew the consequences.

"That was 2 years ago, I've learnt from my mistakes. I give you my word I won't put myself or anyone in danger ever again. I trust these people, more than you know-"

"Do you have any idea how people looked down at us before, the rumours that went around. People blamed us for being bad parents, and now you want to go and join a club full of people who are doing the wrong thing." I gulped as my dad lashed out on me. He rarely spoke but when he did, he could shake the entire family. Talking back was probably the worst thing that I could have done in this situation, but I wanted them to know that I was serious. But the main reason that I was doing this was because, thought of not being able to see him ever again was terrifying.

"Please just this once. All I want is to be able to talk to the people who understand me. Everyone at that club is a friend of mine, I don't want to stop seeing them. You guys weren't there for me when I needed you, but they were, and now you just expect me to leave them. I am sorry that our family wasn't perfect because of my sexuality, but you can't expect me to hide it. "

"Noah, I can't allow you to go to a club that is constantly going to be hated and attacked. Not only am I worried that you will never be normal again if you keep meeting people like that but also about your own safety. So, if you want you can talk to a few of your gay friends, but only occasionally and never in this house. Are we clear?"

I nod my head yes. I don't know whether to be happy or to be furious at them. It was like they said yes and no to what I asked at the same time. A part of me was relaxed, because I was able to tell them everything that I wanted to. It was like releasing something that I had been holding on for so long, each day the weight of it getting heavier. And even though they still weren't ready to accept me, I had still broken down some of the walls they built.

I look towards my sister; she has a huge smile on her face. Seeing her being so proud of me was all that I could ever ask for.

"Good job, kid." Her proud smile grows wider. "I wouldn't even imagine about standing up to them, it's good to see you were able to."

"Thanks," I say, "for everything."

Mark. I have to tell him. All I can think about how I can finally talk to him and spend time, without worrying about what would happen if my parents saw us. I run out the door as fast as I can towards school. It's ironic how I was running away from that place when I first moved here and now it was the only place I wanted to go. The wind brushes against face, it felt like I was finally free. Swerving around the thousands of unfamiliar faces, I finally reach my classroom. Looking around the room, I don't see him. The seat that belonged to him was empty and my heart sank. Maybe he's just late, or maybe he's on his way. He will come. He has to come. I try to convince myself that I was just overreacting and that he was absolutely okay. There was this unsettling feeling in my stomach that was hard to ignore, like something happened to him.

"Noah?" A girl from my class stood in front of me. I couldn't remember her name, but I remember seeing her in the pride club a few weeks ago.

"Yeah. Do I know you?" I asked puzzled by the random conversation.

"Not really. I am a friend of Mark's. I don't think he's coming to school today, or for few weeks. However, he wanted me to give this letter to you." She says handing me a small yellow envelope with my name written on it.

"Thanks." I take the letter from her hands. Once she leaves, I open the envelope and start reading the letter. It seems to be written in a haste; the writing barely legible.

Hey Noah, I know this is probably very confusing. I don't have a lot of time, I'm leaving. I should have told you before, but I didn't want to ruin the little time that we had together. The past few months with you have been the highlights of life. I just want you to know that I wouldn't take back any of it. From the first day that I saw you sitting alone in a corner, I knew that I wanted you to be a part of my life. Anyways, I feel like I owe you an explanation for this. My father didn't know that I was gay, and I never wanted to tell him. The other day when I took you to the pride club, he got to know. His first reaction was to send me as far away from you as he could, so that's what he did. I have a few minutes to pack my things before he sends me to a hostel. I probably won't be able to talk to you for a few years, but I really hope this letter reaches you. Promise me that you'll wait for me, even if I never make it back.

Love, Mark.

I force back the tears that threaten to fall. I couldn't believe what I was reading. Just like that he was gone, without a proper goodbye, without letting me see him, and without a chance for me to tell him how I feel. The class empties out, but I remain there in my seat with the letter in my hand now stained with tears. I felt as though a huge rock had pierced through me, leaving a hole that couldn't be filled. I know that it was beyond my control, but I still wish I could have done something to make him stay, or at least not been the reason he had to go.

He was gone just like that. We didn't get to have a beginning or even a proper ending.

9 798889 862116

Printed by Libri Plureos GmbH in Hamburg,
Germany